SHIVERWOOD ACADEMY
PAIN IN THE NECK

Spellbound
An Imprint of Magic Wagon
abdobooks.com

by Lea Taddonio

To Jarah, Bronte and Poppy–I love you all best – LT

abdobooks.com

Published by Magic Wagon, a division of ABDO, PO Box 398166,
Minneapolis, Minnesota 55439. Copyright © 2020 by Abdo
Consulting Group, Inc. International copyrights reserved in all
countries. No part of this book may be reproduced in any form
without written permission from the publisher. Spellbound™ is
a trademark and logo of Magic Wagon.

Printed in the United States of America, North Mankato,
Minnesota.
052019
092019

THIS BOOK CONTAINS
RECYCLED MATERIALS

Written by Lea Taddonio
Edited by Bridget O'Brien
Art Directed by Candice Keimig

Library of Congress Control Number: 2018964646

Publisher's Cataloging-in-Publication Data

Names: Taddonio, Lea, author.
Title: Pain in the neck / by Lea Taddonio.
Description: Minneapolis, Minnesota : Magic Wagon, 2020. | Series: Shiverwood academy
Summary: Colin Drak is the dud in his family because he hasn't gotten his fangs yet, and
    decides to run away to the human world.
Identifiers: ISBN 9781532135040 (lib. bdg.) | ISBN 9781532135644 (ebook) | ISBN
    9781532135941 (Read-to-Me ebook)
Subjects: LCSH: Vampires--Juvenile fiction. | Fangs--Juvenile fiction. | Runaway children-
    -Juvenile fiction. | Self-acceptance --Juvenile fiction. | Family relationships--Juvenile
    fiction.
Classification: DDC [Fic]--dc23

TABLE OF CONTENTS

Chapter One
THE DUD 4

Chapter Two
THE DOOR IN THE WALL 14

Chapter Three
THE HUMAN WORLD 28

Chapter Four
BACK WHERE WE BELONG 38

Chapter One

THE DUD

It's my first night at Shiverwood Academy and it already **stinks** worse than zombie breath. My twin sisters, Hester and Echo, **BLOCK** the front gate.

"Listen up, you big baby." Hester's fangs **GLEAM**. "I don't care what Mom said before we left the castle. Don't *talk* to us at school. Not in the hallway. Not in the lunchroom. Not at recess."

Echo nods. *If you break these rules, we will tell everyone that you don't even sleep in a COFFIN yet.*

Echo never speaks. But that doesn't mean she is quiet. Her **POWER** is mind talking. And she never shuts up.

Her eyes turn ruby red. *I heard that.*

Did I mention that Echo isn't just a mind talker? She is also a mind reader. It's such a *PAIN*.

Hester sniffs. "And most importantly . . . don't go into Coven Hall. Only **full** vampires have classes there."

Full vampires like my **BiG** sisters.

Hester already has FANGS. And
Mom and Dad say Echo is gifted.
Me? I'm Colin Drak ... the
DUD. The disappointment.
The Draks are an old magical
family who've scared humans for
a thousand years. I'm the only
Drak ever to dislike blood.

I mean, who has ever **HEARD** of a vampire who'd rather drink orange juice?

After my sisters run off, I **trudge** to the building off to one side and glare at the sign:

Misfit Hall

Not fitting in can be a real *PAIN* in the neck. Sometimes I *wish* that I could be a human. Yeah. I bet in the human world everything would be better.

Chapter Two
THE DOOR IN THE WALL

My classroom is in the basement of Misfit Hall. It's hard to pay attention. Instead, I *doodle* bats and ghosts on my History of the UNDEAD worksheet. I can't wait for this stupid night to be over.

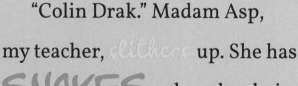

"Colin Drak." Madam Asp, my teacher, slithers up. She has SNAKES where her hair should be. "I just asked you a question."

Ugh. **BUSTED**. My cheeks turn redder than a pair of demon horns.

The other students SNICKER.

"Hey dude!" one kid **YELLS**.
"I've flushed goldfish down the
toilet who're smarter than you."

"Good **BURN**!" His buddy
gives him a high five.

Everyone **laughs** harder
except for the cute red-haired girl
in the front row. She gives me a
look of *pity*. But that is even worse.

The clock above the door

STRIKES midnight.

"Saved by the bell," Madam

Asp *hisses*. "Run along for

recess, everyone."

I don't want to play by myself.

I'm the last one out of the room.

But just before I go upstairs, I hear
a **CREAK**.

CREE

I turn around and a mysterious-looking door is open. I walk over and peer inside.

All I see is a black tunnel.

My heart pounds. I hate the dark. But I hate being a MISFIT more. Maybe this is a way to escape school.

I remember how my mom says, "Colin, you can't **RUN** away from your problems."

But I want to try. So I take a deep breath and **STEP** inside. Next thing I know, I'm running as fast as I can.

Chapter Three
THE HUMAN WORLD

The **tunnel** veers right. Then it veers left. My head spins. At last, a prick of **LIGHT** appears ahead. Finally... a way out.

I **RUN** out through a hole in a spooky tree. How the heck did I end up in this old graveyard?

Ugh. I'm getting out of here.

I **RUN** to the front entrance and

see an old man walking his dog.

"Excuse me," I *CALL* out.

"Can you tell me where I am?"

His fluffy dog **BARKS** and the old man runs away screaming.

I look around and am ready to scream too. Who is behind me? A scary **MONSTER**?

There is *giggling* behind
a headstone.

My big sister Echo STEPS
out from the shadows. *Hello, Colin.*

I hear her voice in my head. *You wanted to see if the human world was better. Here is your*  *chance.*

"Whoa." I look around. "The
human world." My sister must
have heard my *wish* earlier. "Why
did that old man run away?"

She **SHRUGGED**. *Why don't you say hi to someone else and see what happens?*

"Good idea." I *look* across the street. I spot a teenager throwing a trash bag out in front of a house.

"Hey!" I say, walking over.

"Nice night, huh?"

"What the . . ." The teen's eyes BULGE out. "Mom! Dad! Police! *HELP*!" She flees, her arms waving over her head.

"Great. No one likes me here either!" I hate that my eyes fill with tears. Echo will laugh at me.

Chapter Four

BACK WHERE WE BELONG

Here. Take a look*.* Echo pulls her special vampire mirror out of her pocket.

I blink at my reflection. I see my black hair. My red eyes. My light green skin. It's just . . . me.

You're a vampire. Echo slings an arm around my shoulders. *Even if you'd rather drink orange juice than* blood.

"Even if I don't like COFFINS

and I don't have FANGS yet?"

Dad says you'll be a late

BLOOMER, just like him.

"Dad got FANGS late too?"

Hope fills me.

Yeah. He said he had to go to Misfit

Hall for two whole years.

That makes me **FEEL** a lot

better.

1873

1872

Echo gives me a light **PUNCH** on the arm. *You might be a misfit but you are the best artist in the family. Plus I can hear thoughts, and yours are always kind.*

A warm *FEELING* spreads through my chest. "Hey. Should we get back to school? Recess is probably almost over."

Echo gives me a **BIG** hug.
Good idea. Madam Asp hates it when kids are late.

"Let's race! Last one back is a **rotten** dragon's egg."

We go through the **tunnel** to get back where we belong.

I might not be a **PERFECT** vampire. But I'm me. And maybe that's pretty cool after all.